Disney · PIXAR
Inside Out

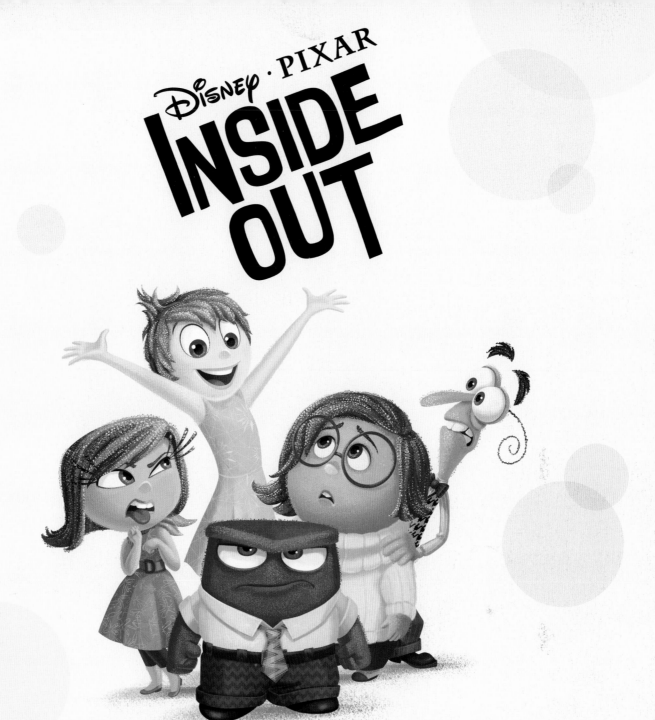

Adapted by Suzanne Francis
Illustrated by the Disney Storybook Art Team

A GOLDEN BOOK · NEW YORK

randomhousekids.com

ISBN 978-0-7364-3313-6

Printed in the United States of America

10 9 8 7 6 5 4 3 2 1

As a lively little girl, Riley was
always on the move. There was a whole world
bustling with activity inside her mind, and
Headquarters was at the heart of it all.
From there, Riley's **Five Emotions** watched
each day unfold for their favorite girl.

Riley's lead Emotion, Joy, loved Riley more than anything and worked day and night to help her have the best life possible. The sight of **happy yellow memories** rolling through Headquarters let Joy know she was doing a good job.

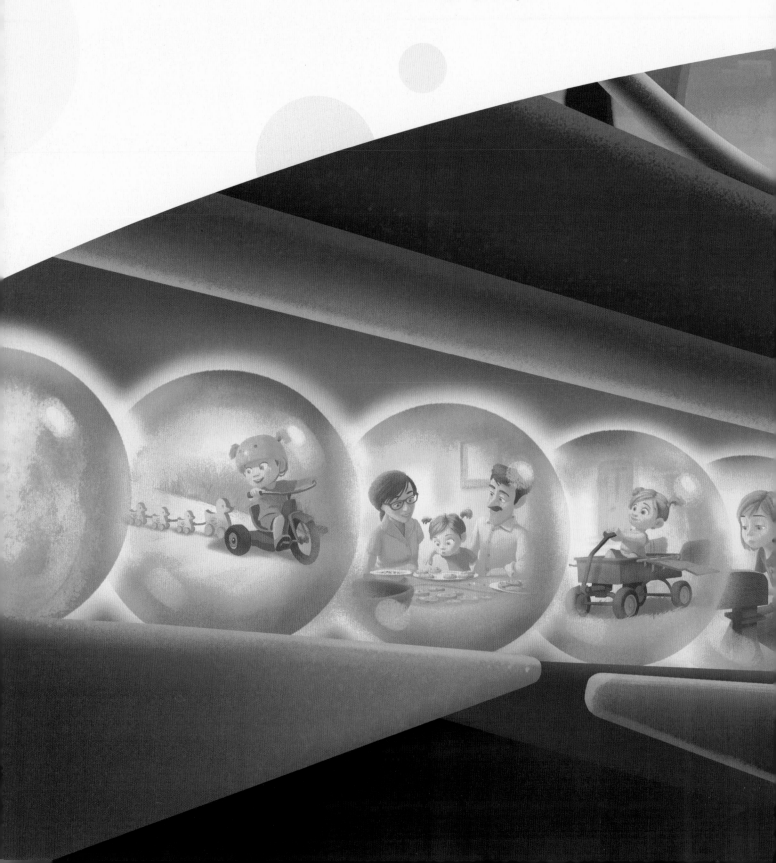

Joy liked being in control, but she understood why Riley occasionally needed her other Emotions, too.
Well, most of them, anyway . . .

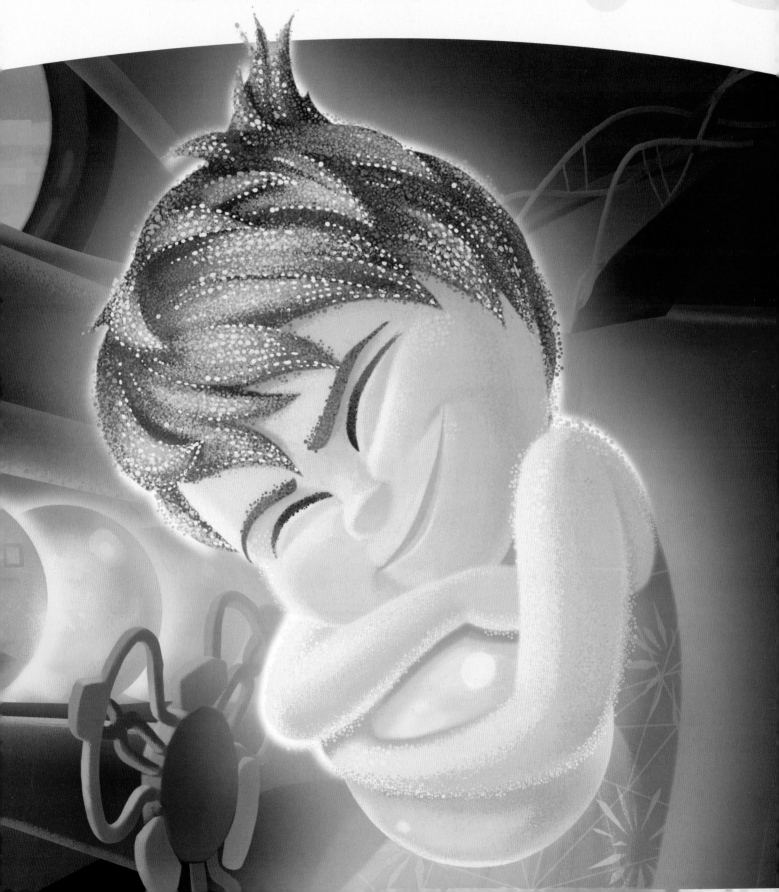

For example, **Riley needed Fear to stay safe**.
Be it power cords or puppies, whenever Riley faced a potential hazard, Fear was there to carefully guide her out of danger.

And of course, **Riley needed Disgust's good taste to avoid being poisoned**, both physically and socially. Disgust helped Riley steer clear of anything and everything she found repulsive, from horrible food to rotten people.

When Riley faced something unfair, **Anger was there to right every wrong**. With his loud growls and well-placed scowls, Anger fought Riley's battles like a pro. And if he got really mad, flames shot out of his head!

Then there was Sadness.

Joy had no idea why Riley needed Sadness. All she seemed to do was make Riley feel gloomy, and Joy never wanted that! So, naturally, Joy tried her best to keep Sadness as far away from the controls as possible.

All of Riley's memories were important. But her **five core memories**—formed from the biggest moments in her life—were *VERY* important. Core memories powered Riley's **Islands of Personality**. Family Island, Honesty Island, Hockey Island, Friendship Island, and Goofball Island made Riley who she was.

For years, Joy successfully ran Headquarters and **Riley had a great childhood**. Most of her memories were a happy shade of yellow, and her Islands of Personality thrived.

But when Riley was eleven years old, her parents made a surprising decision that **changed everything**.

The family moved across the country from Minnesota to **San Francisco**! But the bustling city wasn't anything like Riley and her Emotions expected.

"I don't want to live here," Sadness whimpered when they pulled up to Riley's new home.

"It's the worst," Disgust agreed. "The absolute worst."

"**This house stinks!**" Anger declared.

"San Francisco is terrible," said Fear.

Joy was determined to keep Riley happy. She had an idea for how to turn things around, so she plugged a lightbulb into the console.

All Five Emotions watched as Riley challenged her parents to a game of living-room hockey. **Soon, the whole family was having fun!**

Joy always seemed to make things better.

Later, as Riley laughed about a happy memory of her dad from their road trip to San Francisco, her smile suddenly faded.

Sadness had turned the memory blue!

"What did you do?" Joy asked.

"I just touched it," Sadness said nervously.

No matter how hard Joy tried, Riley's happy yellow memory remained a sad blue one.

Joy ordered Sadness not to touch any more of Riley's memories, but Sadness didn't listen. She accidentally knocked one of Riley's core memories out of the holder!

Without its core memory, **Goofball Island went dark**!

Joy quickly put the core memory back in place before Sadness could turn it blue. Goofball Island came back to life! Joy was worried, though. She needed to keep Sadness away from Riley's happy memories.

The next morning, Joy sprang into action before anyone else was
awake. She wanted to make sure Riley had a great first day at her new
school, and she had the perfect plan to keep Sadness out of the way.
   "This is the Circle of Sadness," Joy explained. "Your job is to
make sure that all the sadness stays inside it."

At school, Riley's new teacher asked her to introduce herself to the class. Riley handled it well at first, but when she started sharing a happy memory from her life in Minnesota, she became homesick. In Headquarters, **Sadness was touching the memory!** Then things went from bad to worse: Riley cried in front of the whole class! A new **blue core memory** rolled into Headquarters!

Joy tried to get rid of the blue memory by sending it up the vacuum tube and out into the Mind World, but Sadness wouldn't let her. During the struggle, Joy and Sadness dislodged the core memories from their holder!

Riley's Islands of Personality went dark!
As Joy raced around trying to make things right, the powerful vacuum tube sucked her up and out of Headquarters, with Sadness and all of Riley's core memories right behind her!

Joy and Sadness rocketed through the tube and landed with a thud on a cliff overlooking the Mind World.

"We can fix this," Joy told Sadness. "We just have to get back to Headquarters, plug the core memories in, and Riley will be back to normal."

Joy and Sadness ran to Goofball Island. Then they began to cross the lightline, which was like a narrow power cord that connected the island to the core memory holder in Headquarters.

Things were not looking good for Riley or her remaining Emotions.
"Great," Anger grumbled. "We have no core memories, no
personality islands, and no Joy."

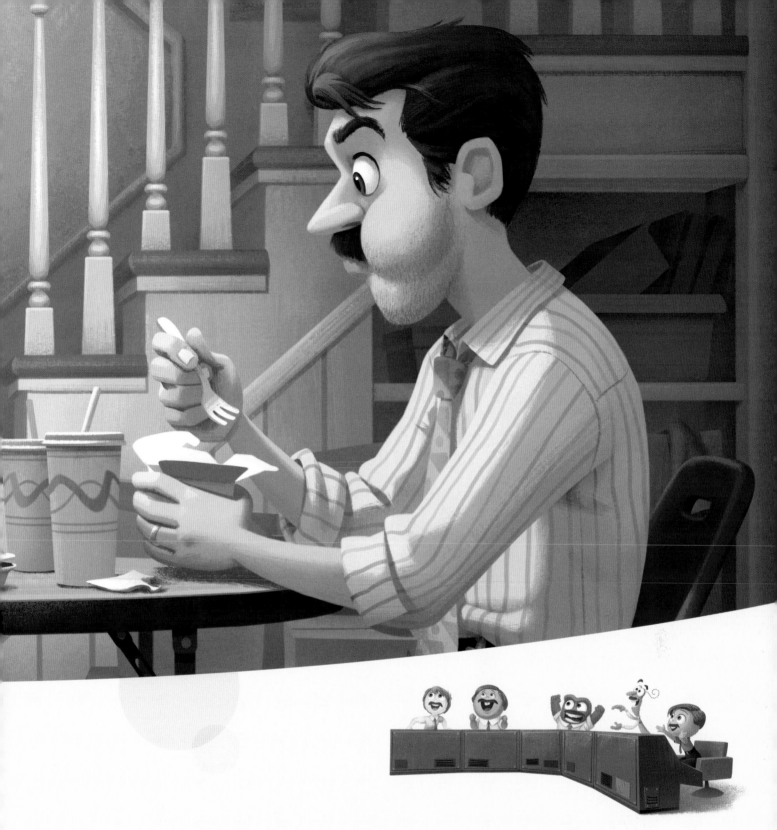

They tried running things themselves, but it was a disaster.
During dinner, Riley's parents noticed her strange behavior, and
their Emotions scrambled to figure out what was going on.
It wasn't long before Riley was sent to her room.

When Riley ignored her dad's attempts to cheer her up later that evening, **Goofball Island started to fall apart!**

As the island crumbled, Joy and Sadness dashed back to solid ground. Together, the two Emotions watched Goofball Island collapse into the abyss. **Sadness was too overwhelmed to move.**

But Joy refused to delay their journey back to Headquarters any longer. She grabbed Sadness's foot and dragged her into the labyrinth of **Long Term Memory**.

As Joy and Sadness meandered through the winding shelves of
Long Term Memory, they came across two **Forgetters**. It was the
Forgetters' job to vacuum up the old memories that Riley no longer
needed and send them down to the **Memory Dump**.

"Nothing comes back from the dump," one Forgetter explained.

Joy was horrified at the thought of throwing away Riley's perfectly good memories, but the Forgetters explained that they needed to vacuum up old memories to make room for Riley's new memories.

The following morning, Riley video-chatted with Meg, her best friend from Minnesota. When Meg told Riley about a new girl on the hockey team, **Riley got upset**.

"Oh, she did NOT just say that!" snapped Disgust.

"A NEW GIRL?" Fear asked in disbelief. "Meg has a new friend already?!"

Anger quickly took charge of the situation.

"I gotta go!" Riley interjected, cutting the conversation short.

As Riley slammed her laptop closed, Friendship Island started to groan and creak.

Back in the Mind World, Joy ran toward the terrible sound.
Friendship Island disintegrated into the Memory Dump.
"That was your favorite," said Sadness. "And now it's gone."
Joy could think only of getting back to Headquarters to help
Riley. She had no choice but to return to the maze of Long Term
Memory, dragging Sadness behind her.

Along the way, the two Emotions ran into Riley's old imaginary friend, **Bing Bong**. Bing Bong was part cat, part elephant, and part dolphin—but he was made entirely of cotton candy.

It had been years since he and Riley had played together. They used to go on **amazing adventures**—mostly in Bing Bong's rocket wagon, which could fly when they sang a special song.

"There's not much call for imaginary friends lately," said Bing Bong with a sigh.

He handed his magical, bottomless bag to Joy so she could carry Riley's core memories safely. Then he told them they could take the **Train of Thought** back to Headquarters.

On their way to the train station, Bing Bong gave Joy and Sadness a tour of **Imagination Land**.

They admired Trophy Town, explored French Fry Forest, and floated through Cloud Town!

"Is it all going to be so interactive?" Sadness asked as Joy and Bing Bong leaped across lava with glee.

They even saw some new parts of Imagination Land, like the Imaginary Boyfriend Generator. **Joy was not impressed.**

Meanwhile, Riley was trying out for her new San Francisco hockey team. But without Hockey Island running, she was having a hard time.

Fear tried to jam old hockey memories into the core memory holder to power up the dark island, but it spit them out. **Riley made so many mistakes** that she got frustrated and stormed off the ice!

Crash! **Hockey Island fell to pieces.**

Back in Imagination Land, Bing Bong cried candy tears: **Mind Workers had thrown his rocket wagon into the Memory Dump.**

Joy tried to cheer him up, unsuccessfully. But when Sadness sat beside him and listened, he started to feel better.

Joy was baffled. **How could Sadness have made Bing Bong feel better?**

She didn't have time to give it a second thought, though, because Riley had fallen asleep. They needed to wake her up so the Train of Thought could take them back to Headquarters.

Thankfully, Sadness spotted **Dream Productions**. Perhaps a lively dream would do the trick?

"Okay, how are we gonna wake her up?" Joy asked Sadness as they walked through Dream Productions.

Sadness thought a **nightmare** would work best, but Joy didn't like that idea at all. She wanted Riley to wake up from **sheer happiness**.

Joy found a dog costume nearby and handed half to Sadness.
"Riley loves dogs!" said Joy. "Put this on!"
With Bing Bong's help, Joy and Sadness made a big scene on set.
"Let's party!" Joy shouted between barks. "Let's dance!"

In Headquarters, Fear was on **Dream Duty**. He watched Riley's dream of a dog playfully barking on-screen. But when Joy and Sadness accidentally ripped the costume in half, it looked completely real! **Fear was terrified!**

Sadness pointed at the sleep indicator. Scaring Riley was working—she was waking up! But before they could do anything else, the dream director called security.

Sadness, Joy, and Bing Bong ended up in the **Subconscious**, where Riley's deepest fears were kept—like Grandma's vacuum and **Jangles the birthday clown**.

Joy realized then that Sadness's original plan to scare Riley awake was their best bet. So she led Jangles out of the Subconscious and onto the Dream Productions set.

The sight of the giant clown created a **terrifying nightmare** that instantly jolted Riley awake!

Back at Headquarters, **Anger had an idea**. He thought that if
Riley ran away, back to Minnesota, all their problems would be solved.
"Who's with me?" he asked.

Disgust and Fear agreed, so Anger boldly plugged the idea bulb
into the console.

Meanwhile, on the Train of Thought, Bing Bong picked up one of Riley's memory spheres. It was Joy's favorite: Riley's afternoon by the twisty tree in Minnesota with her mom, dad, and hockey team. **To Joy's surprise, it was Sadness's favorite memory, too!**

Of course, Sadness liked the sad part of the memory—Riley's team had just lost the big playoff game.

"Riley missed the winning shot. She felt awful," Sadness explained.

Joy sighed. She had thought for a moment that Sadness was finally looking on the bright side of things.

At home, Riley stole her mom's credit card to pay for a bus ticket back to Minnesota. **Riley's actions caused Honesty Island to crumble**, and the debris crashed onto the train tracks!

Workers frantically helped everyone off as the Train of Thought fell to the dump below.

"We lost another island!" Joy cried. "What is happening?"

A worker broke the bad news: **"Riley is running away."**

Joy, Sadness, and Bing Bong scrambled toward Family Island. It was the only island still standing.

But as Riley left the house to run away, Family Island started to fall apart, too!

In the chaos that followed, both **Joy and Bing Bong plummeted into the Memory Dump**, leaving Sadness stranded on a cliff.

Joy and Bing Bong felt hopeless as Riley's memories dissolved into mist around them. Joy cried as she watched the twisty tree memory again. She thought about what Sadness had said. Suddenly, something dawned on her.

"Mom and Dad . . . the team . . . they came to help because of Sadness."

Joy finally understood the importance of feeling sad and realized that **Riley really did need Sadness!**

"We have to get back up there!" Joy declared.

By singing Bing Bong's special song, Joy and Bing Bong managed to find his rocket wagon so they could fly up and out of the dump!

They raced down a mountain of old memories, **singing their hearts out to get the rocket to fly**. It shot into the air—but not high enough to reach the cliff above the Memory Dump.

"Come on, Joy, one more time!" Bing Bong said as he noticed his hand starting to fade. "I've got a feeling about this one."

They raced down the hill **one last time**, singing together and gaining momentum.

"Louder! Louder, Joy!" Bing Bong shouted. "Sing louder!"

Then, without Joy noticing, **Bing Bong jumped out of the rocket**.

The rocket flew higher and higher, until . . .

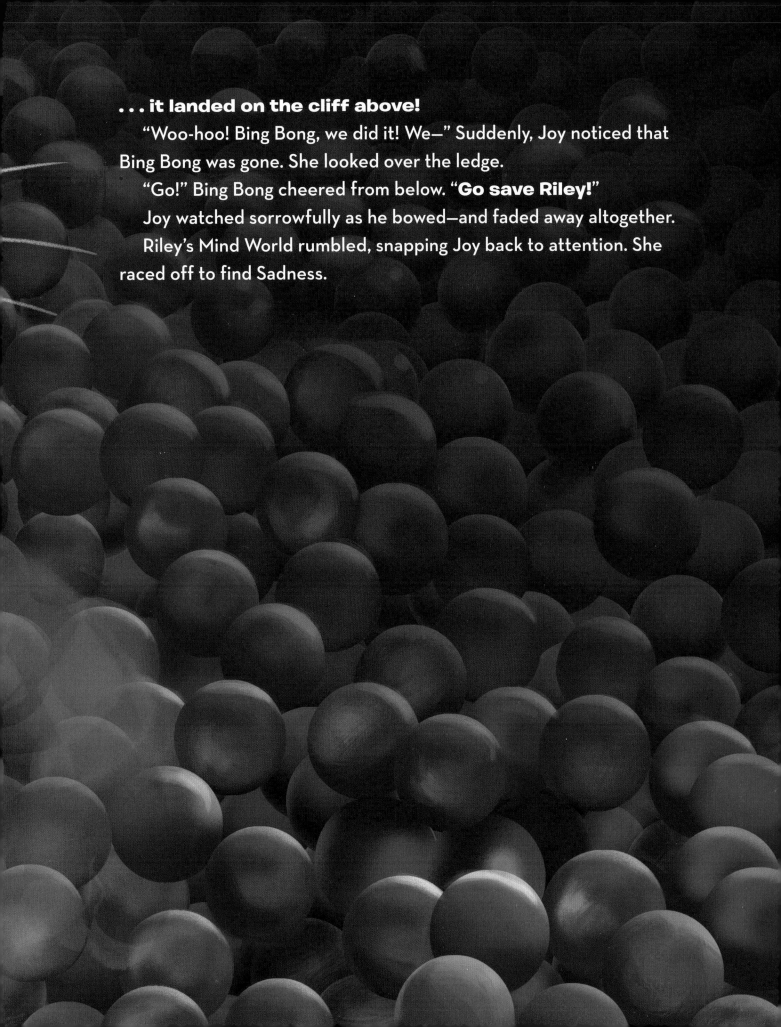

. . . it landed on the cliff above!

"Woo-hoo! Bing Bong, we did it! We—" Suddenly, Joy noticed that Bing Bong was gone. She looked over the ledge.

"Go!" Bing Bong cheered from below. "**Go save Riley!**"

Joy watched sorrowfully as he bowed—and faded away altogether.

Riley's Mind World rumbled, snapping Joy back to attention. She raced off to find Sadness.

Meanwhile, Sadness was floating away on a cloud from Cloud Town!

"**I only make everything worse!**" she cried as Joy chased after her.

Suddenly, Joy had a crazy idea. Using the Imaginary Boyfriend Generator, she created a tower of boyfriends and stood at the very top.

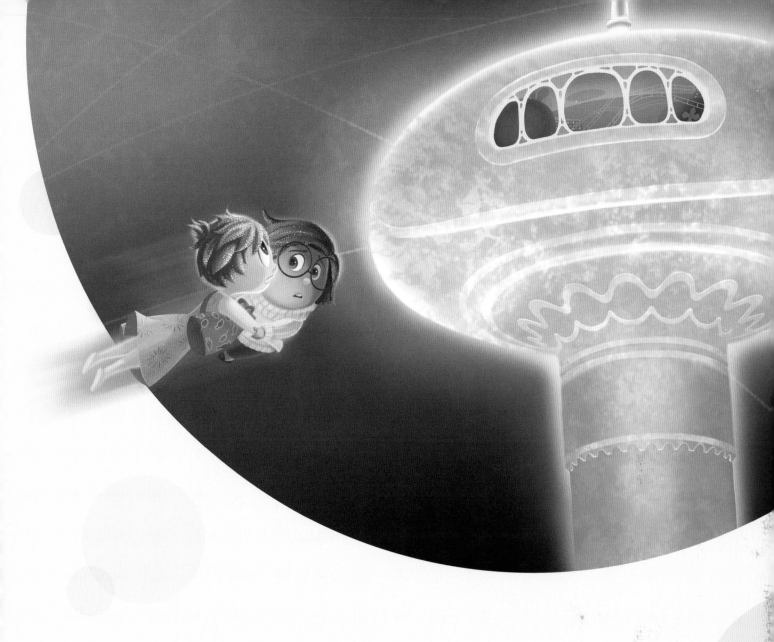

"**NOW!**" Joy shouted as the boyfriends launched her to a trampoline on Family Island. She bounced up and caught Sadness in midair! The two soared across the sky and smacked right into the windows of Headquarters! **But how could they get inside?**

Disgust had a plan! She made Anger REALLY mad and used him like a blowtorch to cut a hole in the glass. Joy and Sadness quickly climbed through.

Reunited, all Five Emotions watched as Riley got onto the bus. "Sadness, it's up to you," Joy said.

"Me?" Sadness hesitated. "I can't, Joy."

Joy gently pushed Sadness toward the console. "Yes, you can. Riley needs you," she said. "Now go."

Sadness touched the console, and **Riley began to feel really sad**. She thought about her parents and felt even sadder. She wanted to be with them.

"Wait! Stop!" Riley shouted to the bus driver, rising from her seat. "I wanna get off."

Riley jumped off the bus and raced back home.

Sadness helped Riley talk to her parents and tell them how she
really felt.

"I know you don't want me to, but . . . **I miss home**," Riley said
through her tears. "**I miss Minnesota.**"

"I miss Minnesota, too," Dad replied. "I miss the woods where we
took hikes."

"And the backyard where you used to play," added Mom.

Riley's parents understood. **It was okay to be sad.**
Then they hugged her tight and Riley knew that even though things
were hard right now, **everything was going to be just fine.**

It wasn't long before Riley was enjoying her life in San Francisco. **With new interests and friends came new core memories and new Islands of Personality.**

Riley was growing and changing every day. But no matter what happened, Joy, Sadness, Fear, Anger, and Disgust would always be with her, helping her through each day **as a team.**